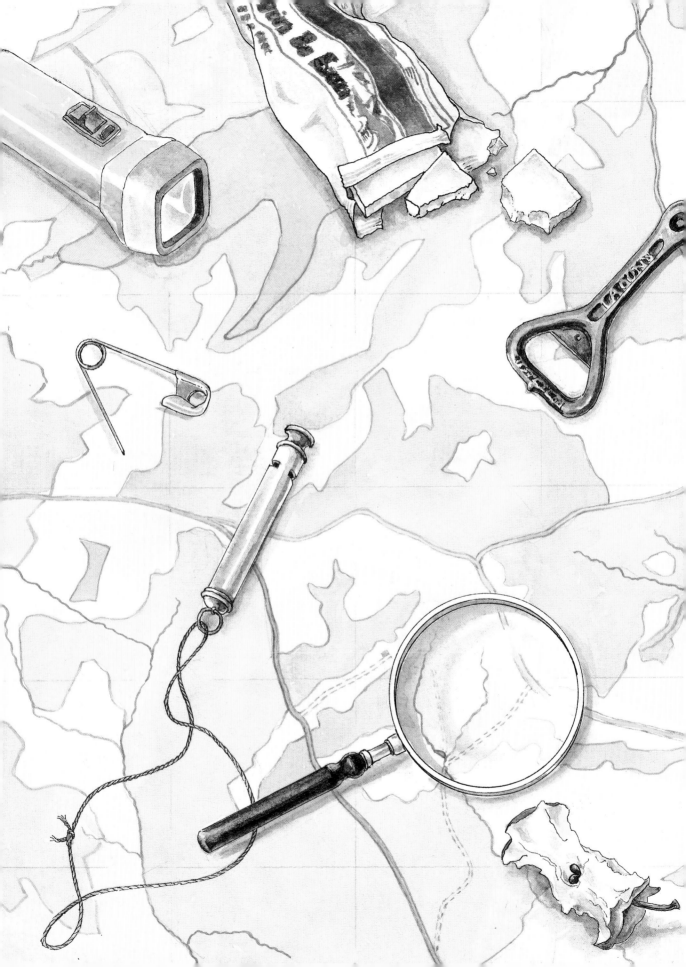

For Karl

Copyright © Prue Theobalds 1990

First published in 1990 by
Blackie and Son Limited
7 Leicester Place, London WC2H 7BP

British Library Cataloguing in Publication Data
Theobalds, Prue, 1936 –
     The teddy bears' great expedition.
     I. Title
     823'.914 [J]

     ISBN 0-216-92896-6
     ISBN 0-216-92993-8 Pbk

First American edition published in 1990 by
Peter Bedrick Books
2112 Broadway, New York, NY 10023

Library of Congress Cataloging-in-Publication Data
Theobalds, Prue.
   The Teddy bears' great expedition / Prue Theobalds. — 1st
   American ed.
        p.   cm.
     Summary: Colonel Gruff leads a group of teddy bears
   on an expedition to discover the real, live bear that may be their
   ancestor.
     ISBN 0-87226-425-4
     [1. Teddy bears—Fiction. 2. Bears—Fiction. 3. Safaris—
   Fiction.] I. Title.
   PZ7.T3523Te 1990
   [E] —dc20

Printed in Hong Kong by Wing King Tong Co. Ltd.

The Teddy Bears'
Great Expedition

Prue Theobalds

Blackie
London

Bedrick/Blackie
New York

'BEARS WANTED,' the notice read, 'for expedition
to be led by Colonel Gruff, intrepid explorer, to
find a wild bear, Ursus Arctos, the ancestor of the teddy bear.

Wear clothing suitable for all weathers. Bring camping
gear and plenty of provisions.

The expedition will leave Thursday next, sharp at nine
o'clock.

Those wishing to take part please sign below.'

The word was quickly spread around.
    Bears of all shapes and sizes, old and young, patched and bald, thin and stout came to sign their names.

On Thursday next by nine o'clock
there was a great gathering of bears,
all suitably dressed and well equipped
with rucksacks, tents, ropes, compasses,
binoculars, tins of bully beef, bars of
chocolate and bottles of ginger beer.

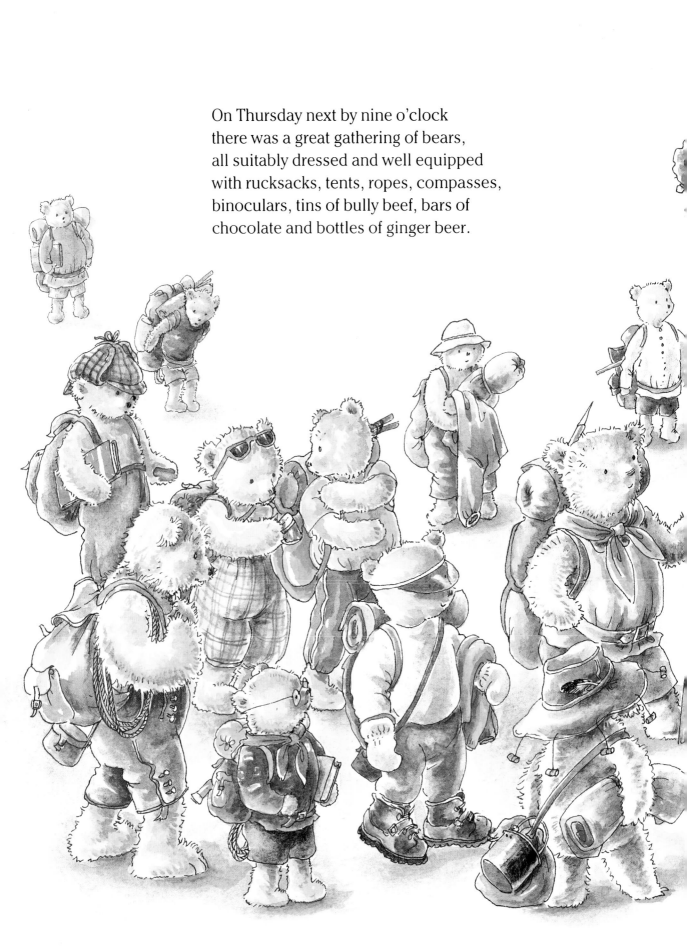

The Colonel called them all to order.

'Right!' he said, showing them a large map. 'We will take a course 10°NNE SW to this forest which, in my experience, is the place to look for a large plantigrade mammal.

Follow me and no fooling about. THIS IS A SERIOUS EXPEDITION!'

All the bears fell in line eager to start the great trek.
They walked and walked and walked and walked!
They reached the forest – and still they walked.
'Please Sir, can't we rest?'
'Please Sir, I'm hungry!'
But the smallest bear said, 'Please Sir, we have
passed that tree three times!'

'Ahem! I was just checking the lie of the land,' said the
Colonel.

'Sh! What's that sound?'

They could hear a rustling and a snuffling and a
thumping.

'It's a bear!'

'A BEAR!'

'WHERE?'

'Hide – it's THERE!'

But it wasn't a bear.

That night they camped by a river.

'In my experience,' said the Colonel, 'this is just the place where bears will come down in the night to drink. We must take it in turns to keep watch. You five will volunteer.'

'Oh Sir!'

'All night, Sir?'

'Can we have extra rations, Sir?'

'I'm afraid of the dark, Sir!'

But the smallest bear said, 'Please Sir, shouldn't we camouflage the tents?'

It was getting darker and darker when SUDDENLY
there was a squelching and a splashing and a snorting!
'What IS that there?'
'There is something HUGE in the river!'
'Quick, get a torch!'
'Ouch! My foot!'
'I KNOW IT'S A BEAR.'

But it wasn't a bear.

The next day the Colonel studied the horizon with his binoculars.
'In my experience,' he said, 'bears live in caves on high ground.'
'That's a MOUNTAIN, Sir!'
'I don't like heights, Sir!'
But the Colonel was off – 'Follow me, no lagging.
Remember THIS IS A SERIOUS EXPEDITION.'

Higher and higher they climbed.

'I'm cold, Sir!'

'I'm scared, Sir!'

'I'm feeling sick, Sir!'

But the smallest bear said, 'Please Sir, shouldn't we be roped together?'

'Just what I was going to say,' said the Colonel.

He roped them together and they put on their gloves and scarves and set off again. Higher and higher they went.

They came round a crag and there in the snow were tracks!
'Sir! Here are tracks!'
'Where do they go?'
'To a bear's lair!'
'It's THERE – OH NO!'

But it wasn't a bear.

Coming down the mountain was faster and more fun than
climbing up.
'BEHAVE YOURSELVES!' shouted the Colonel.

'Here we have Elephant Grass and in my experience it is just the kind of place to find bears.'

'Or elephants,' said the smallest bear.

But the Colonel did not hear. He had disappeared into the tall grass and all they could see was the top of his hat.

With a sigh and a moan they followed him, trampling the grass down as they went.

SUDDENLY they stopped in their tracks!

'What was that terrible noise?'
Was it a bark or a howl or a bray or a growl?
'IT COULD ONLY BE A BEAR!'

But it wasn't a bear.

They all flopped down.
'I'm tired, Sir!'
'Where else can we look, Sir?'
'Can't we go home, Sir?'

But the smallest bear who was reading a book said,
'Please Sir, it says here that the British wild bear is extinct!
It died out in the eleventh century so we are 900 years too late.
The only place we will find a bear now is the zoo.'
    'Just what I was going to suggest,' said the Colonel.
'Come on, I'll lead the way.'

They found the zoo and there at last was a REAL LIVE BEAR. It was large, with claws and a lot of hair and looked rather bored.

It peered at them with a kindly, enquiring expression. The Colonel coughed and said, 'Hello,' and explained why they had come. The bear seemed very pleased to meet them.

URSUS ARCTOS

And the smallest bear said, 'Well it HAS been a successful expedition after all.'